A CHOOSE YOUR OWN ADVENTURE® BOOK

SPACE HAWKS™

ALIEN INVADERS

Book 2

W9-CCQ-877

By Edward Packard

Illustrated by Dave Cockrum

BANTAM BOOKS
NEW YORK • TORONTO • LONDON • SYDNEY • AUCKLAND

RL 5, age 10 and up

ALIEN INVADERS

A Bantam Book / August 1991

Cover and interior illustrations by Dave Cockrum
Colors by Judith Fast

ISBN 0-553-28839-3

Published simultaneously in the United States and Canada

Bantam Books are published by Bantam Books, a division of
Bantam Doubleday Dell Publishing Group, Inc. Its trademark,
consisting of the words "Bantam Books" and the portrayal of a
rooster, is Registered in U.S. Patent and Trademark Office and
in other countries. Marca Registrada. Bantam Books, 666 Fifth
Avenue, New York, New York 10103.

PRINTED IN THE UNITED STATES OF AMERICA
OPM   0 9 8 7 6 5 4 3 2 1

You Are a Space Hawk— Are You Ready To Meet Your Next Challenge?

"The swarm is about seven billion miles across, roughly the same diameter as our solar system," Commander Bradford says. "The number of Cephids has now been calculated at close to a trillion."

Several Hawks whistle out loud.

"These creatures vary in size—the average is about the size of the largest dinosaur that ever lived."

Pete Walton gets to his feet. As the squadron leader, he calls the shots when the Hawks are out on a mission.

"With all due respect, Commander," he says, "I don't see what even the Space Hawks can do against a trillion Cephids. We could shoot them down all day, every day, for months, and there would still be billions of them that would get through."

"You're right," Bradford says. "But remember, you Space Hawks weren't selected just because you could outshoot everyone else. You're supposed to be able to *outthink* everyone else. Your mission is to find out what else we can do!"

YOU'VE ALREADY GOT ONE MISSION UNDER YOUR BELT— BUT WAS THAT JUST BEGINNER'S LUCK? *YOU* DECIDE.

Bantam Books in the Choose Your Own Adventure® series
Ask your bookseller for the books you have missed

ALIEN INVADERS

Your Mission

The year is 2102. The nations of our world are at peace, and a united Earth Federation has been formed to govern our planet. But new dangers await humankind. Alien life-forms have recently been detected in outer space, posing a serious threat to the planet Earth.

In response to this challenge, the Earth Federation has formed a squadron of twelve top astronauts, each of whom flies one of the fantastic new Phantoms, the first spacecraft with faster-than-light capability. These extraordinary pilots are called Space Hawks. Their mission is to protect the people of Earth from alien invasion, and to meet the unexpected challenges of the cosmos. After a rigorous competition, you were chosen to be one of them.

In your previous adventure, you and the other members of your squadron helped to end a civil war on the planet Baakra. Now a much greater challenge awaits you. The Cephids—a horde of enormous insectlike creatures—are moving toward Earth, destroying everything in their path.

You'll have to think fast and act quickly, because you'll be in situations unlike any on Earth. From time to time as you read along in this book, you will be asked to make a choice. After you make your decision, follow the instructions to see what happens next. What happens is up to you. If you survive, you'll be in for the greatest thrills and adventures of your life.

Good wishes and good luck.

You and your pals, Norie Kiasaka and Alto Bay, are perched on the high pontoon of a catamaran, racing toward the Hawaiian beach.

A brisk west wind has whipped up the waves on the dazzling blue sea. The sun is smiling down on you, and the warm salt spray is flying in your face.

Alto's from Kenya. A member of the Maasai tribe, he holds two Olympic gold medals for track.

Norie's from Japan. She's so tiny she almost didn't qualify for Space Hawks training. Still, she's one of the best pilots in the squadron.

It's been a great day sailing, and you're feeling really happy. You never have more fun than when you're with the Space Hawks. In addition to being the best pilots in the galaxy, they really know how to have a good time!

The catamaran suddenly picks up speed as a gust of wind hits it.

"This is fantastic!" Norie shouts.

"Wha-hoo!" Alto yells. "It's like riding a charging elephant!"

"Watch it!" Norie yells.

→ → → → → → → → → → → → → → → →

Go on to the next page.

2

A huge wave, bigger than any before it, lifts the catamaran higher and higher. A strong gust of wind catches the sail. The catamaran heels dangerously. You tighten your grip on the tiller—a big wave could capsize the boat. "Slacken the sheet, Alto!" you yell.

Alto eases the sail.

"The beach is coming up fast!" Norie shouts.

Suddenly you're riding through the breaking surf.

"Get your weight back, everyone!" As you yell these words, the catamaran sails through the air. The surf breaks beaneath it.

The three of you leap out into the wash of the breaker and haul the boat onto the beach.

You've landed on the big island of Hawaii, where the Space Hawks—the most elite squadron in the galaxy—is based. A glance at your watch tells you that the fun's over for the day. You're due for a meeting in just thirty minutes.

During the months ahead, you're not likely to do much sailing. Brock Bradford, the Space Hawks commander, has summoned the entire squadron for a briefing on a crisis facing the Earth Federation.

Almost a year has passed since you first learned about the Cephids, a horde of monstrous insectlike creatures that are sweeping through space like a swarm of locusts, destroying every planet in their path. You'll never forget the moment you heard about them.

You had just become one of the twelve Space Hawks. You were vacationing on a beach in Oahu when you got a call summoning you to headquarters. A few hours later you were on your first mission—a journey to the planet Baakra.

You and four of the other Space Hawks had your hands full trying to get the red- and the green-furred Baakrans to end their civil war. It wasn't easy. You got caught in the middle of their battle, and your career as a Space Hawk almost ended right on the spot! All the while it wasn't just the furry creatures of Baakra you were worried about. As Commander Bradford said, "If the Cephids overrun Baakra, Earth will be next."

→ → → → → → → → → → → → → → → →

Go on to the next page.

Now a year has passed. Though the Baakrans successfully ended their civil war and began to prepare themselves for the onslaught of the Cephids, they may have started too late. The computers are predicting that the Cephids are just months away from reaching Baakra, and its inhabitants may not be able to stave off the invaders, even with help from the Space Hawks!

The briefing room at Space Hawks Headquarters is filled promptly at 5:00 P.M. All twelve Hawks are there. Some, like Alto and Norie, you've seen a good deal during your vacation. Others, like Pete Walton and Rapper McCoy, who flew with you on the mission to Baakra, spent their time climbing mountains in Tibet.

Pete is your squadron leader. He may be older than the other Hawks, but he can still keep up with the best of them. He comes from Tennessee and talks in an easygoing way, yet he's smarter than anyone you ever met.

Rapper's from Australia. He used to be a road racer, and has a three-inch scar across his face from an accident. He likes to tell people that he quit road racing because cars were too dangerous for him—as if flying a Phantom spacecraft were any safer!

→ → → → → → → → → → → → → → → →

Go on to the next page.

6

Although you've met all of the Space Hawks, there are still several Hawks you haven't gotten to know well. They are some of the most intelligent and skillful pilots who ever flew in space, and they come from all over the world.

Commander Brock Bradford holds up his hands to get everyone's attention. He's standing on the stage at the front of the room. A Mark VII holographic projector is mounted beside him.

"Welcome back, Space Hawks! I'm glad to see everyone's looking healthy and rested. In the weeks ahead we're going to have our work cut out for us. Our entire solar system is facing a challenge that threatens its very existence. Latest reports from our observatories indicate that the Cephids are still heading for Baakra. And they'll be heading for us next."

Bradford presses a button, and a holographic projection appears at the far end of the room—a computer-generated three-dimensional map of space spanning a ten-light-year radius from the Earth. The sun is a bright point of light in the center of the projection. It's surrounded by its nine planets, represented by other tiny points of light. The scale is distorted in order to show the nearby stars.

As you know from your studies, there are only eight stars within ten light years of the sun. Two of them are even brighter than our own sun. One is Alpha Centauri, the closest visible star; the other is Sirius, the "Dog Star," the brightest star in the heavens. Neither of these mighty stars have any known planets that can support life. Among the other nearby stars, only one, Barnard's star, has been discovered to have a set of planets; and only on one of these, Baakra, has intelligent life been found.

There is nothing in this projection that comes as a surprise to you—you've seen it all many times while you were in training. But then Bradford touches another button, and a startling sight appears—a swarm of tiny specks moves through space, heading toward Baakra.

→ → → → → → → → → → → → → → → →

Go on to the next page.

9

The swarm of Cephids appears to move through the galaxy. An electronic calendar displays the date moving ahead, day by day. The swarm reaches Baakra just as the calendar records the passage of sixty-three days from today. Then the calendar is sped up. Weeks instead of days move by, and the swarm appears to move much more swiftly—heading straight toward Earth!

"This is a computer simulation," Bradford says. "It may be off by a few days, but not by much."

He switches off the projection and turns up the lights in the room. You look around at the other Hawks. Like you, everyone seems stunned by the demonstration.

"How big is the swarm?" asks Igor Denisov, a Russian member of the Space Hawks. "How many of these Cephids are there?"

"The swarm is about seven billion miles across, roughly the same diameter as our solar system," Bradford answers. "The number of Cephids has now been calculated at close to a trillion."

Several Hawks whistle out loud.

"These creatures vary in size—the average is about the size of the largest dinosaur that ever lived."

→ → → → → → → → → → → → → → →

Go on to the next page.

"How much gravitational force do they exert?" you ask.

Bradford directs a sharp eye at you. "Good question, Hawk 3. If the Cephids weighed as much as a dinosaur, their combined weight might exert enough gravitational force to pull the Earth out of its orbit. But, strangely, these creatures, or whatever they are, don't seem to weigh much more than a few pounds each. Some scientists speculate that they are made of mostly *energy.*"

Pete Walton gets to his feet. As the squadron leader, he calls the shots when the Hawks are out on a mission. Although he likes to kid around, everyone respects him, and the room becomes absolutely silent.

"With all due respect, Commander," Pete says, "maybe the Space Hawks could knock off a billion or so Cephids, but a trillion? We could shoot all day, every day, for months, and there would still be billions that would get through."

"And we'd run out of laser propellant way before that." Everyone looks around at Stefan Svensen, the Norwegian member of the Space Hawks, and an expert on laser weaponry.

"You're right," Bradford says. "But remember, you Space Hawks weren't selected just because you could outshoot everyone else. You're supposed to be able to *outthink* everyone else. If we just squared off and tried to fight it out with the

Cephids, of course we'd be wiped out. That's why your mission is to find out what else we can do!"

Everyone starts talking at once.

Bradford holds up his hand.

"I'm going to divide our forces into three groups," he says. "Each of you will have a separate mission. I expect you to report back to Earth within thirty days."

He pulls out a sheet of paper. "Team A will proceed to the planet Baakra and help the fur creatures prepare their defenses. There's a chance that our combined forces might wreak enough havoc among the approaching Cephids to drive them away from the planet. The Baakrans may have developed some defense strategies already. We'll soon find out.

"Team B will proceed directly to the leading edge of the Cephid cloud," Bradford continues. "Your goal is not to attack, but to find out as much information about the Cephids as you can, like what they are and how they behave. I want to know their strengths and their weaknesses. Are they a single intelligence, or do they act independently? Are they capable of reason? Who directs them? We need to learn a lot more about them than we now know."

→ → → → → → → → → → → → → → → →

Go on to the next page.

The commander pauses a moment. He consults a computer monitor and touches a button. A pinprick of red light appears in the holographic projection. A scale shows that it represents an object located about seventeen light years from Earth on a bearing of about 90 degrees from Baakra.

"That's the destination of Team C," Bradford says. "We've named it 'Gamma One.' Our astronomers at Mauna Kea detected it only a few weeks ago. It emits irregular signals to the Cephids using a highly sophisticated code that we've been unable to break so far. We believe it's an artificial radio source—a radio transmitter floating in space, perhaps inside a spaceship of some kind, but perhaps not."

Norie Kiasaka speaks up. "If Gamma One controls the Cephids, and we can control *it*, then—"

"Exactly," Bradford interrupts. "But we mustn't think we can just cruise alongside and turn this thing on or off. If some higher intelligence did place a radio beacon there, and they're using it to control the Cephids, then you can be sure it's very well protected."

"Is there any chance of breaking the radio code?" you ask.

"We have an array of supercomputers working on it," the commander replies, "but you mustn't expect quick solutions." Then, in a grave tone of voice, he adds, "You have to understand—more

than likely we're dealing with an intelligence higher than our own."

"Then how do we have a chance?" Stefan asks.

"We have a chance because we're Space Hawks!" Bradford's voice rings out.

→ → → → → → → → → → → → → → →

Go on to the next page.

No one says anything for a moment. You wonder if the others feel the same tingling in their spines that you feel.

"I want all of you to meet back here tomorrow morning at 8:00 A.M. sharp," Bradford says, "and let me know which team you wish to volunteer for. The order in which assignments will be given will be decided by lottery, so give some thought to what your first choice will be, and also your second choice."

That night you lose quite a bit of sleep trying to reach a decision.

→ → → → → → → → → → → → → → → →

If your first choice is to join Team A, going to Baakra, turn to page 28.

If your first choice is to join Team B, going to probe the Cephid cloud, turn to page 17.

If your first choice is to join Team C, going to probe the radio source Gamma One, turn to page 105.

You ignite your port burners, then gently add on starboard retros. The Phantom swerves violently to starboard, and you black out. When you come to, you see the attacking Cephid falling back on your port quarter.

You read the data coming up on the screen. The Cephid was able to maneuver only slightly from its original course while the Phantom was making a very tight turn. The Cephid reminds you of a charging rhinoceros—massive, deadly, and fast, but not very agile.

You adjust your controls and set a new course, still cruising along the edge of the swarm. You're feeling a little better knowing that the Phantoms can run rings around the Cephids—until you remember that the Earth Federation has just twelve Phantoms, and there are about a trillion Cephids!

You travel eight minutes more—about six hundred thousand miles—when you see a tiny, stray comet, one that must have escaped from the gravitational field of its sun. It's headed right for the Cephids!

→ → → → → → → → → → → → → → → →

Turn to page 27.

Only two days have passed since your meeting at Space Hawks Headquarters. The lottery completed, you're now in deep space, on your way to probe the Cephid swarm. You're flying in formation with the other members of Team B, Pete Walton, Alto Bay, and two Hawks you haven't flown with before. One is Maria Marquez, who comes from Bogotá, Colombia; the other is Sedge Jennings, from Cornwall, England.

Maria, whose complexion is dark, has silky black hair and is descended on one side of her family from the Incas. Her family members were llama breeders, and she grew up in a stone cottage on the side of a mountain three miles above sea level. You've hardly gotten to know Maria, but you're impressed with her quick thinking and her sense of humor.

Sedge Jennings is tall and lean. When you first met him he seemed a bit snobby, but the more you see of him the more you like him.

Right now you're several billion miles from Earth, approaching the outer limit of the solar system. From this distance the sun looks like just another superbrilliant star.

→ → → → → → → → → → → → → → → →

Go on to the next page.

Your on-board computer has locked onto the swarm of Cephids, seven light years away. You can see them on your display screen. They appear to be moving through space very slowly, but you know they're really traveling extremely fast.

As you pass the orbit of Pluto, the voice of Pete Walton comes over your earphones.

"All right, Hawks, prepare for FTL transit in six minutes. We'll rendezvous directly in the path of the Cephid swarm at the coordinates I'm patching into your computers. At that point the leading edge of the swarm will be only several hundred million miles away. From then on we'll maneuver at sublight speed."

One after another the voices of the other Hawks come across. "Acknowledged—preparing for transit."

You run a last check on your FTL system, then press your speaker button. "Hawk 3 ready."

Developing FTL, faster-than-light, transportation was one of the supreme technological achievements of all time. Although nothing can actually travel faster than light, the Phantom spacecraft can achieve almost the same thing by boring a wormhole through space-time, allowing it to emerge almost instantaneously in another place in the galaxy. The process isn't easy. Performing the necessary steps requires a level of skill that few pilots could ever attain.

FASTER THAN LIGHT...

The six-minute preparation period is now complete. A tingling feeling surrounds your body, then you're pulled into another state of being as you fall unconscious.

→ → → → → → → → → → → → → → →

Go on to the next page.

Slowly you come to, blurry eyed and slightly confused. Your eyes fix on one of your video monitors. It shows a large area of space almost completely blocked out—with only a little starlight coming through. Focusing on the huge dark area, you see for the first time the telescopic enlargements of the Cephids. They are spaced so that each one is between three and four miles from its nearest neighbor. The entire swarm is hundreds of millions of miles across.

The Cephids don't really look like insects, as you had thought they would, but more like fantastic crabs, with huge flattened bodies over a hundred feet long, and with spiked pincers that extend far out ahead of them. All too clearly you can see their tooth-filled jaws, larger than even a shark's.

Another monitor displays the four other Phantoms in your team. Everyone made it safely through space-time. You're thankful for that; there's always a chance of a mishap since the technology of FTL travel isn't really fully understood. It relies on quantum mechanics, an area of science where things happen that seem illogical, or impossible.

"We're all here," Pete Walton announces. "But it looks like we'd need a thousand Space Hawks to make a dent in this horde."

"Now I know how Winston Churchill felt before the Battle of Britain," Sedge Jennings puts

in. "His main weapon was *courage.*"

"Yeah, but the British won that battle," Alto replies, "and I don't see how we're going to win this one."

→ → → → → → → → → → → → → → →

Go on to the next page.

"We're going to find out soon, or get out of here," you say. "My computer shows that the swarm is traveling at a quarter of light speed. That means they'll reach us in less than half an hour."

"Twenty-two minutes," reports Maria Marquez with the precise calculation.

Pete comes back on. "All right, everyone, fan out and cruise along the edge of the cloud—*formation-12.* Don't open fire except in self-defense. We've got to learn more about these creatures before we can do anything. Rendezvous back here in five hours."

"Will do," you say into your mike. At the same time you ignite two afterburners and peel off to starboard. In a moment the other Phantoms are just blips on the screen behind you.

You're closing in on the Cephids at an oblique angle. The nearest ones grow larger on your display screen. You study their gigantic pincers and their enormous mouths, always opening and closing. You test for electronic transmissions, but as far as you can tell, the Cephids are silent. They may be receiving transmissions from Gamma One at this very moment, but you can't really tell.

An hour has passed. The nearest Cephids are eight million miles away. A touch of your afterburners and a slight adjustment on the rudder

brings your Phantom onto an almost parallel course with the swarm. At this range you can begin to make out some individual differences among the Cephids. Some of them are a good deal larger than others, some differ in shape.

→ → → → → → → → → → → → → → → → →

Go on to the next page.

Six minutes later—you're only eight hundred thousand miles from the nearest Cephids. With your optical enhancers you can see detail as if they were only a few hundred yards away. But nothing gives you a clue on how to deal with these creatures. It scares you to think what will happen if they ever reach Earth.

Your Phantom's laser cannon can fire thirty devastating laser blasts, or one gigantic "magnum" blast, before it needs to return to an energy source for recharging. Powerful as your weapon is, it could only take out one Cephid at a time, since they are spaced so widely apart. That means you could destroy about thirty of these monsters at most—thirty in a swarm of a trillion! You'd have about as much effect against them as a mosquito attacking a herd of elephants! Obviously, if the Space Hawks are going to turn back the Cephids it won't be with fire power alone.

Range is now just sixty-five hundred miles to the nearest Cephid. You wonder if they are aware of your presence.

Suddenly your question is answered. The Cephid closest to you has left the swarm, and is accelerating directly toward you!

Your instructions are to fire only in self defense. Well, maybe this is one of those times. You alert your computer with a voice command.

"Lock on approaching target and prepare to fire on command—full-force power."

You watch the Cephid racing toward you, rapidly growing larger on the screen. Should you maneuver to avoid it, or fire?

← ← ← ← ← ← ← ← ← ← ← ← ← ←

If you maneuver to avoid the Cephid,
turn to page 15.

→ → → → → → → → → → → → → → →

If you fire, turn to page 30.

You slow down and adjust your course so you can watch what happens. You don't have long to wait. When the comet comes within about twelve hundred miles of the swarm, the Cephid nearest to it suddenly accelerates, shifting direction into a collision course with the comet. A few moments later you witness a tremendous explosion as the comet and the Cephid collide.

Well, that's one less Cephid, you think. But then you see the neighboring Cephids racing directly toward the explosion, ignoring the heat and the blast coming toward them! For a moment a blueish-white halo of light obscures the scene. As it fades, you see that the Cephid hit by the comet is still there, and now it's grown much larger! Its enormous pincers are waving violently, as if energized by the explosion!

→ → → → → → → → → → → → → → → →

Turn to page 29.

The next morning you arrive at the briefing room with your first and second choices ready. Commander Bradford asks everyone to draw a card out of a deck. You draw the three of diamonds, the lowest card of anyone.

Well, you've been pretty lucky so far. There was no reason to think it would keep up forever. Now you won't get your first choice. You'll have to go for your second choice.

← ← ← ← ← ← ← ← ← ← ← ← ← ← ←

If your second choice was to join Team B, going to probe the Cephid cloud, turn page 17.

→ → → → → → → → → → → → → → → →

If your second choice was to join Team C, going to probe the radio source Gamma One, turn to page 105.

The other Cephids pass the point of the explosion, while the one that was hit—by now twice as big as the others—suddenly veers toward you.

You hit the emergency evasion button. The computer ignites both starboard burners. The Phantom accelerates into a tight curve. By the time you come out of it, you're half a million miles from the nearest Cephids.

You can breathe a little easier now. At the same time you're in a state of shock over what you've seen. If that comet had collided with Earth, it would have made a crater fifty miles across. Yet not only was the Cephid unharmed by the impact, but it grew in size and power and speed!

There can be only one explanation for what you've just seen. These creatures thrive on energy, even when it's directed at them with terrific force!

You ponder this terrible truth as you alter course and head back for the rendezvous with the other Hawks.

→ → → → → → → → → → → → → → → →

Turn to page 35.

"Fire!" Your computer responds to your voice signal, sending out a stream of intense blue-white light that strikes the Cephid square on. For a few moments a blinding halo obscures the action—bright yellow-white at first, then changing to red, then violet—before fading away.

Your jaw falls open. The Cephid is still there! What's more, it's grown larger. And now it's accelerating toward you!

What kind of creature is this? You don't have much time to think about it—it's coming faster than ever!

You've got to act quickly. You can try to get away, or you can continue to fire, hoping to destroy the creature.

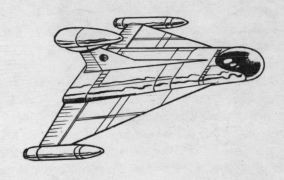

→ → → → → → → → → → → → → → →

If you let loose with multiple bursts from your laser cannon, turn to page 49.

If you try an emergency evasion maneuver, turn to page 33.

32

You volunteer for the mission to the space fortress of the Fiber People. The next morning you report to Commander Bradford's office.

"You come across as a person of sincerity and goodwill," he says. "I think you'll make a fine ambassador."

You feel yourself blush when you hear these kind words. "Thank you, Commander. I appreciate your confidence."

Bradford smiles back, but then his face quickly turns serious. "Of course we can't be sure that these good qualities—ones that would make you an excellent ambassador on any mission among Earthlings—will have the same effect on some alien race. We must remind ourselves that other creatures in the universe may not only *look* different than Earthlings, they may *think* differently also."

"I understand that, sir," you say. "We learned a lot about interspecies communication at the space academy. Doctor Vivaldi taught us that there's a lot more to understanding aliens than just translating their words."

"Exactly," Bradford says. "And that's particularly true when the aliens are more advanced than we are. And it seems likely that that's the case with the Fiber People."

→ → → → → → → → → → → → → → → →

Turn to page 52.

"**E**mergency evasion maneuver!" you command. Luckily you don't have to give details. The computer already knows the course, speed, and rate of acceleration of the oncoming Cephid.

The Phantom's starboard burners ignite. An emergency booster kicks in. You're blacked out by the g-forces for a few moments. When you come to, the Cephid is far behind.

→ → → → → → → → → → → → → → → →

Go on to the next page.

You've escaped, and you've learned that with skill and care the Phantom can evade these monstrous creatures. But you've also learned that the Cephids feed directly on energy. Instead of destroying them, firepower makes them grow larger, faster, and stronger.

With this frightening knowledge, you alter course, eager to rendezvous with the other Hawks.

As you near the edge of the swarm, you monitor the vast numbers of Cephids that you pass. None of them seems to have received any recent inputs. As far as you can tell, they are all just plodding along through space, waiting for an energy burst to arouse them.

A tiny object shows up on your radar screen. For a moment you think it might be a meteor, but then you realize that it's traveling in the same direction and at about the same speed as the Cephids.

You zoom in toward it, putting your optical scope on maximum gain. As you approach within a few hundred miles, a clear picture emerges on your screen. The object is not a meteor, but a tiny Cephid, barely five feet across. It's like a baby that strayed from the rest of its herd.

Here's a great opportunity. If you could capture this tiny Cephid and bring it back to Earth for study, scientists might learn how to control these creatures.

Quickly you alter course and carefully approach the tiny creature. It continues on, apparently unaware of the Phantom's approach.

→ → → → → → → → → → → → → → → →

Go on to the next page.

Meanwhile you keep an eye on the leading edge of the swarm. If the baby has a mother and it figures out what's happening, you're likely to have your hands full.

You coast toward the little creature. Just as baby animals on Earth are always cute, no matter how they will look when they grow up, so is this baby, though its pincers could surely twist your arm off.

When you're right alongside it, you open the outer hatch, and maneuver sideways, hoping the creature will slide right in.

Almost . . . almost . . .

You apply a microburst of power from the lateral thrusters.

"Ah-ha!" you say aloud. The video monitor shows that the tiny Cephid has slid into the Phantom's air lock. You press the button and close the outer hatch. A second later your capture is complete; the Cephid is floating securely in the air-lock chamber.

You watch it on the video monitor. The way it's nuzzling the electrical paneling makes you uneasy. It must sense a source of energy there. Suppose it bites through?

You can feel the sweat breaking out on your brow. This may not have been such a smart idea.

You accelerate, throwing the baby Cephid back against the bulkhead. Now it's just lying there, stunned. You put the Phantom on autopilot and go back into the air lock, securing the Cephid in restraints and bracing it with air bags so it won't get hurt as the Phantom maneuvers. Then you radio a report to Pete Walton and head for the rendezvous point. Within twenty minutes you're closing in on the others.

"This is Hawk 3. I've got the rest of you on my screen now," you say into the mike. "Retrofiring into formation."

"Glad you're back, Hawk 3," Pete answers. "Patch in your detailed report for unified display."

→ → → → → → → → → → → → → → → →

Go on to the next page.

You touch a button, transmitting your report to the display screens of the other Hawks. A moment later the reports of the others come up on your screen.

ALTO BAY—HAWK 2: I got pretty close to the edge of the swarm. One of these things came after me, but I lit a couple of extra burners and took off.

SEDGE JENNINGS—HAWK 4: My orders were not to fire on them, but I did want to have a bit of sport. I fired off a Mark V space flare. The flare carried deep into the swarm. Several Cephids went after it. One of them snapped it up. It was as if I threw bait into a school of fish!

PETE WALTON—HAWK 1: I saw Cephids, some the size of elephants, others five times as big as that. The nearest one accelerated toward me. I fired in self-defense. Instead of blowing up, it grew larger, then kicked its speed up so fast I had to get out of there in a hurry.

Before you can read Maria's report, Pete Walton motions with the fins on his spacecraft, trying to get your attention. Then you hear his voice. "Hawk 3—amazing work!"

"Nice going, Hawk 3," Maria cuts in. "I can't wait to see what one of those babies looks like up close."

"That was something, Hawk 3," Sedge Jennings says. "But we mustn't go soft on these monsters."

"That's a good point," you say. "A baby Cephid may look cute, but as we've found out, they're quite deadly."

"There's no need to feel discouraged," Pete Walton says. "Now that we've captured one of these creatures, we have to get it back to Earth fast and have our scientists study it. Once we've figured out what the Cephids are all about, we'll have some idea how to deal with them. Prepare for FTL transit. Follow standard procedures and rendezvous in stationary Earth orbit over Oahu."

When you hear this, you apply the space-time coordinates for immediate return to Earth.

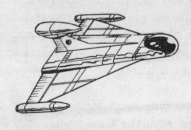

→ → → → → → → → → → → → → → → →

Go on to the next page.

Yours is the first of the Team B Phantoms to set down at Space Hawks Headquarters in Hawaii. You've radioed ahead about having a baby Cephid on board—you just hope Earth scientists will know what to do with it once they receive it.

The first thing you do when you land is to check the video monitor trained on the air lock. The Cephid is clawing away at the hatch, like some huge crab trying to get out of a box. It seems none the worse for wear.

A Hovercraft skims over the runway. It pulls up alongside your Phantom, and Commander Bradford steps out, along with other men and women whom you don't recognize. Another Hovercraft follows, then a big van, two military trucks, and a heavily armored tank! The baby Cephid is getting quite a reception. You open the canopy and leap down to the tarmac.

Bradford shakes your hand and congratulates you on your work. He introduces you to the people he's brought with him, scientists and technicians, including two zoologists, two chemists, and Doctor Bruno Vivaldi, whom you've heard lecture at the space academy.

The scientists take turns climbing into the pilot's compartment of the Phantom and observing the baby Cephid on the video monitor. Then they meet on the tarmac and question you for details.

Commander Bradford motions for the van to pull up next to the Phantom. At this moment you hear a roar over by the far end of the airfield. Another Phantom is coming in for a landing. Bradford is too fascinated with the baby Cephid to even look up.

"Here's our plan," Doctor Vivaldi says after the scientists finish their discussion. "We'll back the van up to the hatch of the Phantom and build a little bridge between the two. Then we'll shine a very low intensity laser beam from inside the van toward the Cephid. We think the Cephid will move toward the power source when the air lock opens. Once the Cephid is in the van, we'll close that back door. We hope it will then become quiet, and we can transport it to a secure laboratory for further study."

"That sounds like a good plan," you say, "but don't be so sure the Cephid will cooperate."

"I know, but we've got to take certain chances. Besides, we will be prepared for any emergency." Doctor Vivaldi gestures toward the tank. Its forty millimeter laser cannon is pointed directly at the van.

→ → → → → → → → → → → → → → → →

Go on to the next page.

"You do understand that firing at one of these creatures can make matters much worse," you say.

Doctor Vivaldi nods. "We have other methods," he says. "Our zoologists are standing by, prepared to fire tranquilizer darts. We don't know to what extent that will help, if any. But if this Cephid is anything like a wild animal, it will be peacefully sleeping a few seconds after it's hit.

"If that doesn't work," Doctor Vivaldi continues, "we'll have to try to control it by sending powerful electromagnetic impulses into it. Firing a laser cannon at close range will be our last resort."

Brock Bradford, who has been listening to every word, rests a hand on your shoulder. "Now you see why we have some of the top scientists in the world here. The last thing we want to do is to fire a laser cannon at this creature. But I don't think we're going to have to."

"I sure hope you're right," you say.

"It's going to take us a couple of hours to get fully prepared for the Cephid's transfer," Doctor Vivaldi says. "There's no need for you to hang around." His voice is almost drowned out as another Phantom touches down on the runway.

"I'm not tired. I'll be glad to wait in case I could be of any help," you say.

"Sorry," Bradford says. "I know you don't want

to leave the baby Cephid, but we're going to have a meeting at Space Hawks Headquarters in about ten minutes, as soon as the last Phantom is back on the ground. A lot has happened while you were on your mission. Two of our Hawks, Norie and Rapper, are trapped in a force field that surrounds Gamma One. We've got to plan a rescue strategy."

The atmosphere is tense in the Space Hawks briefing room as Brock Bradford programs the holograph projector.

"Our number-one priority right now is to rescue Norie and Rapper," he says. "Our top scientists are working on the best plan of action. Because of the force field, we can't learn anything about Gamma One. What's more, communications are completely cut off from our Hawks trapped inside the field.

"Fortunately, the Hawks on Team A, which went to Baakra, all returned safely. Z'bong, the commander of the red-furs, has led an expedition to take on the Cephids far out in space. Our Space Hawks ambassador, Nick Cracas, warned Z'bong that, if he attacked any Cephids, the rest of them might change course and head right at his planet instead of passing it by. We've urged Z'bong and the other Baakrans to coordinate their efforts with us, but they seem intent on doing things their own way."

"That's right, Commander," Nick Cracas says. "And from what we've now learned about the Cephids—how they gain in size and power from being fired at—the Baakrans' policy is worse than doing nothing!"

"I agree, Commander," you say. "The only hope for Baakra is for us to divert the Cephids from the planet somehow, rather than attack them."

"Maybe we shouldn't help the Baakrans after all," Jack Tyner says. "Maybe we should save our forces for defending Earth."

"I disagree," Alto Bay says. "I think we have a duty to help them any way we can. Remember, Jack, it was the Baakrans who first warned us about the Cephids. If it hadn't been for them, we might not have had time to prepare ourselves."

"Besides," you add, "the Cephids would gather strength and size from consuming additional energy after invading Baakra. If we don't help stop them, it will be harder than ever for us to defeat them."

Others start to chime in, but Bradford raps on the top of the holograph projector. "I want to hear all your ideas before we take action to deal with the Cephids," he says, "but let's get on with our first job, which is to rescue Norie and Rapper from the Gamma One force field. We'll need every remaining Space Hawk to do it."

When the next morning dawns, ten Phantoms are lined up on the tarmac, ready to depart on the rescue mission to Gamma One. You and the other nine pilots have assembled first in the briefing room.

→ → → → → → → → → → → → → → →

Go on to the next page.

"Last evening," Commander Bradford begins, "we received a radio signal from a new group of aliens, ones we weren't even aware of. We've named them the Fiber People. In a moment you'll see why."

Bradford touches a button and a hologram appears before him. It shows a creature shaped very much like a human being, but without any skin, flesh, or bones! More than anything else it looks like those pictures you've seen in anatomy books—a picture of the nerves and muscles of a human being.

"Where did the message come from," Pete Walton asks, "and what was it?"

The commander projects a new hologram that displays a huge, egg-shaped structure against a background of stars. "The message was transmitted from this object."

"Is that a spaceship, sir?" you ask.

Bradford thinks for a moment. "When something's this large," he says at last, "I'm more inclined to call it a space fortress. It's about eleven light years away, and less than one light year away from a very large star that you can see any winter night—Procyon."

"The 'Dog Star,'" Alto says.

"Right. The message we received was not entirely clear. But our chief linguist has translated it as follows."

Earth people: You are taking great risks and are endangering us all by interfering with the radio source you call Gamma One. Do not come near it. You can save your planet by diverting the Cephids, but you must not try to save Baakra.

"We're not going to do as they say, are we?" Pete Walton asks. "If we followed their instructions to stay away from Gamma One, it would mean leaving Norie and Rapper behind."

→ → → → → → → → → → → → → → → →
Go on to the next page.

"We're *not* going to do that!" Alto Bay says in a loud clear voice.

The other Hawks shout their approval.

"Don't worry," Bradford says, holding up his hand for silence. "We're not going to leave our Hawks to die just because of some message from creatures we never even heard of before. I want all but one of you to leave on the rescue mission to Gamma One at dawn tomorrow. I'll need one Hawk to go on a special mission to the space fortress of the Fiber People. Perhaps then we can learn more from them in time to help us against the Cephids. Who would like to volunteer for that mission?"

Before you decide, you quickly review your options.

← ← ← ← ← ← ← ← ← ← ← ← ← ← ← ←
If you volunteer for the mission to the Fiber People's space fortress, turn to page 32.

→ → → → → → → → → → → → → → → →
If you feel it's more important for you to go on the mission to rescue Norie and Rapper, turn to page 67.

"Repeat fire!" you say, giving the voice command to your computer. At the same time you hold down the red *continuous fire* button. You're determined to destroy this Cephid even if it means using all your reserve power.

Once again the target is obscured by a halo of light, this one much brighter, with fierce reddish-orange flames flickering out in all directions. Nothing could survive such an assault.

As the light dissolves, a terrible specter emerges: The Cephid has grown tenfold. Its great mouth is quivering, its enormous pincers almost surrounding you as they close . . .

→ → → → → → → → → → → → → → → →
Go on to the next page.

You call on the Phantom's faster-than-light capability—it's your only chance. "Emergency FTL escape!"

But even as you shout the command into the computer, the Cephid's pincers lock onto your spacecraft, and in one smooth motion you are carried into the creature's enormous mouth.

The End

"It's probably a good thing they are more advanced than we are," you say. "We'll need the benefit of their technology if we're to turn back the Cephids."

Bradford nods. "You may be right."

He glances at the clock on his desk. "Now there's no time to waste. I've asked some top programmers to help you prepare for your mission. They will see that your on-board computer has all the necessary data to plot your course. You'll also have the latest decryptography equipment to help you decipher any signals you may encounter. I want you to be off the ground within forty-eight hours."

Forty-eight hours have passed since your meeting with Commander Bradford, and you're already in deep space, accelerating past Mars. Space Hawks technicians and scientists worked around the clock to prepare you to get off ahead of schedule.

As you cruise through space, you can't help but think about how the other Hawks might fare on their rescue mission without you there to help. It's not a comforting thought, and you try to put it out of your mind. After all, Commander Bradford felt that it was essential to send at least one Phantom on a misison to the Fiber People. And you have no doubt that he was right—the fate of Earth may depend upon your success.

You review your checklist and study your notes on the Fiber People, rereading the strange message they sent, trying to understand their alien minds. Then you lie down to sleep. You'll need to be well rested for what's to come.

Six hours pass, and your wake-up recording, a Scott Joplin piano rag, is playing in your ears. That music always puts you in a good mood.

While you check out your instruments, you drink some pineapple juice, fresh from Hawaii. The Phantom has climbed up to full sublight power, and you're now past the orbit of Saturn.

You put the ship in FTL preparation mode, and begin the six-minute countdown. When the ready light comes on, you remove the guard from the control panel and press the yellow button.

A tingling sensation rushes through your body, and a muted amber light fills the craft. A moment later, you leave space-time.

FASTER THAN LIGHT...

Your brain slowly comes to life, as if you've been in a deep sleep. In a way you have, though not for any measurable length of time, since the Phantom has traveled through a hole in the space-time continuum, passing through some unknown, unknowable region, emerging in another part of space altogether.

Looking through the starboard viewport, you can see the great star Procyon shining like a blue-white beacon.

You begin searching for the Fiber People's space fortress with your optical scope. Within seconds its image appears on your screen—range, a hundred and ten million miles. It's far larger than you'd imagined—almost thirty miles long. It's gigantic, without visible fins, antennae, or engines. More than anything else, it looks like an enormous, perfectly smooth egg.

Slowly you turn the Phantom toward the space fortress. You don't want to do anything that would seem hostile, so you proceed at a very moderate speed. Then you broadcast a message, using basic mathematical ciphers.

Greetings, Fiber People. The spacecraft approaching you, bearing 067-88-D11, is from the planet Earth. We received your message about the Cephids and the radio source Gamma One, but we do not understand it. I have been sent to learn more from you, and bring friendly greetings from all Earthlings.

No reply comes back, but you keep sending the message over and over.

You're certain that the Fiber People are monitoring all frequencies. They must have received your message and are only delaying while they decide what to say.

→ → → → → → → → → → → → → → → →

Go on to the next page.

56

At present speed you will reach the space fortress in about seven hours, but you doubt the Fiber People will let you get that close. More than likely they'll send a delegation out to inspect your craft.

You'd much prefer it if they would let you land. There must be some great hatch that opens and closes in order to let spacecraft in and out.

As you journey steadily closer, you still receive no response. It gives you a spooky feeling. The Fiber People must be watching you—but why don't they communicate?

Four hours have passed since you first sent your message. The space fortress is now less than twenty million miles away, and you've yet to receive a reply. You break out in a cold sweat inside your space suit. You have a terrible feeling that if you get within a certain distance, they may just blast you out of the sky.

Then a message comes through. It takes your computer a few seconds to translate it and bring it up on your screen.

Return to Earth.
You have not been invited here.
Heed this warning.

→ → → → → → → → → → → → → → → →

Turn to page 58.

Your heart sinks when you read this. You'll need time to think. You radio back.

Message received.
Please allow five minutes for reply.

They haven't shot you down yet, so you're pretty sure they'll give you a few minutes more. Still you're so anxious you can hardly think straight. Why would they send a message to Earth, and then not be willing to meet with you? And why is it so important for you to be *invited*? It doesn't make sense.

You begin to feel angry, but then you remember that these aliens not only speak a different language from humans, more than likely they may *think* differently. You can't expect the same behavior from them that you would from Earthlings.

You consider heeding the Fiber People's warning and returning to Earth. But part of you thinks you should continue on and make another plea to land.

→ → → → → → → → → → → → → → → →

If you return to Earth, turn to page 72.

If you decide to continue on, turn to page 62.

The crack in the force field, you realize, is like the eye of a hurricane. All is calm within the eye, yet if you stray outside it, you will be struck by the strongest winds in the storm.

The edge of the crack is marked by powerful magnetic disturbances. To stay safe, you must constantly maneuver your Phantom.

You have your hands so full you don't even have time to search for the trapped Hawks. But then you get another message from Norie.

"Hawk 3, this is Hawk 5. I have you on my radar. Rapper and I are off your starboard bow right above you. We're trying to work our way toward the crack. The turbulence here is terrible."

A second message comes through—this one from Rapper. "Hawk 3, this is Hawk 6. Matey, we're grateful to you—we couldn't have found the crack without you. If it holds open a little longer, we'll be out of here. But you've got to watch yourself. Your position shows that you're getting dangerously near Gamma One."

You acknowledge these transmissions, and try to swing the Phantom back toward the edge of the force field. But your controls aren't responding. You're too close to Gamma One!

You try to alter course, applying emergency thrust, but the added power only increases the magnetic bonds that hold you.

→ → → → → → → → → → → → → → → →

Turn to page 73.

Two days later, less than 125 hours after you left on your mission, your Phantom touches down on the runway at Space Hawks Headquarters in Hawaii.

Commander Bradford is waiting for you on the tarmac. You're not looking forward to telling him about how you failed in your mission. But as you step through the hatch, you let out a joyful whoop—Norie and Rapper are getting out of a Hovercraft nearby. They've been saved from the Gamma One force field!

"It's great to see you!" you yell, as you jog toward them. "Everyone else okay?"

Commander Bradford, Norie and Rapper jerk their thumbs in the air. "It was a bit of a tough time, mate," Rapper says, "but the strategy worked wonderfully. Nine Hawks fired at once, and they were able to open up a crack in the force field. We came out of there like birds flying out of a barn!"

"I wish I had done as well," you say. "I got within a few million miles of the space fortress, but they ordered me to turn back. They said I wasn't invited."

Bradford scowls. "It's unfortunate," he says. "I'm sure we both could have gained a great deal by cooperating with one another."

You recount the details of your mission.

"At least you were able to get some detailed pictures," Norie says. "Maybe our scientists can deduce something from studying them."

"Unfortunately, there's other bad news," Bradford says. "The Cephids have sped up. They're now expected to reach Baakra any day now."

→ → → → → → → → → → → → →

Turn to page 93.

You feel you can't turn back from your mission now, so you continue on toward the space fortress. Slowing your speed even more, you think about what message to send back to the Fiber People. They seemed to think it important that you be *invited* before visiting them. Maybe you can coax them into doing just that. You quickly prepare another message, making it as polite as possible.

> On behalf of the Earth Federation, I respectfully request an invitation to visit your fortress. We need to discuss how to deal with the Cephids. Will you please extend an invitation for me to land?

You read over the message before sending it. You can't be sure it will work, but it's the best you can do. With the push of a button, you direct your computer to transmit it.

Your Phantom continues on toward the space fortress. You wait nervously for a reply.

The minutes tick by. The gigantic egg-shaped object grows larger on your display screen.

650,000 miles away now . . . 625,000 . . . 600,000 . . . Even at this close range, the image in your scope shows no details, no imperfections in the smooth surface of the space fortress.

A message finally comes back.

Turn back at once.
This is your last warning.

You shiver as you read these harsh words, but you didn't get to be a Space Hawk by being scared. You're determined to get these creatures to talk.

In an effort to show your peaceful intent, you slow your Phantom down even more. Then you start to compose a new message. After a few minutes thought, you transmit the following words.

Please reconsider. The Earth Federation needs your help and guidance in dealing with the Cephids. If you have any doubt about our motives, please send out a space-probe to inspect my craft. Your scout could come on board. You will see that my laser cannon is disarmed.

Once again you wait anxiously for the Fiber People's reply.

→ → → → → → → → → → → → → → → →

Go on to the next page.

The minutes tick by. You check the range finder. The space fortress is now less than two hundred thousand miles away, closer than the distance between the Earth and its moon! You can see it clearly with the naked eye now. It looks like a star, growing brighter by the minute.

Suddenly a paralyzing shock surges through your body! The instruments on the control panel quiver wildly. Every alarm and warning light is flashing. As horrible as it feels, you keep thinking, at least I'm still alive!

The Fiber People could have destroyed you, but they didn't. What is their purpose, you wonder. You stare with astonishment at your instruments. Some mysterious force is slowly turning your Phantom around, heading it back toward Earth! Minutes later it is settled on a new course. Suddenly your instruments begin functioning, and your body feels normal once again.

There's no doubt now of the power of the Fiber People, or that they mean what they say. You're thankful, at least, that they didn't blow you to pieces. There's no point in arguing now—the main thing for you to do is to get back to Earth and rejoin the other Space Hawks.

You start the six-minute countdown in preparation for FTL transit, but a malfunction warning light immediately comes on. You groan as you read the words coming up on the display screen.

FTL system inoperative. Impossible to re-
pair without assistance. Only sublight
speed propulsion available.

You don't even bother to ask the computer how
long it would take for you to reach the Earth at
sublight speed. You're eleven light years away.
You know it would take more than eleven years
to get there, that is if you had enough fuel to
build up to maximum acceleration. But you
don't. What's more, your food and oxygen
couldn't possibly last for more than a year.

Dejected, you stare at the words that appear
on your display screen, ones not generated by
your computer.

Earthling, you may safely land on the ninth
planet of Procyon.

This is clearly a message from the Fiber People. Apparently they decided not to abandon
you in space!

→ → → → → → → → → → → → → → → →
Go on to the next page.

Your celestial chart shows that Procyon's ninth planet is less than half a light year away. You ask your computer what data it has on this planet. Within seconds you get the answer.

Procyon Nine is an uncharted planet eight billion miles from its mother star. It is slightly smaller than the Earth and has a habitable atmosphere. It is considered a possible planet for colonization. Federation spaceships have been instructed to inspect it at the earliest possible opportunity. No other data available.

You immediately head your Phantom toward Procyon Nine. There's a good chance you will survive there, and a good chance of being rescued by Earth Federation spaceships—that is, if there are any left after the Cephids attack.

The End

FASTER THAN LIGHT...

You'd like to volunteer for the mission to investigate the Fiber People, but it seems more important for you to try to free Norie and Rapper from the force field surrounding Gamma One.

Most of the other Hawks feel the same way, but it's Stefan Svensen who volunteers for the mission to investigate the Fiber People.

After seeing him off, less than forty-eight hours later you're in the air yourself. You pass through the Earth's atmosphere, then streak toward the outer limits of the solar system, entering FTL mode, bound for Gamma One.

→ → → → → → → → → → → → → → → →

Go on to the next page.

The interstellar transit goes smoothly. All nine Phantoms reenter space-time near Gamma One, just as planned. A preliminary survey reveals that everything is still the same. Norie and Rapper are still trapped inside the force field, but because of electronic interference, it's impossible to pinpoint their exact locations.

Pete Walton comes on the radio.

"All right, partners, we're going to fan out and cruise along the edge of the force field. Look for a break in the skin, a weak point we can penetrate. With a little luck, one of us will find a crack or a rift in the field. If any of you do, let the rest of us know as soon as you can. We'll then rendezvous at the crack, and fire all our laser cannons, concentrating on that one spot. Our combined firepower should open a good-sized tunnel. Two volunteers and I will then fly inside, find Norie and Rapper, and lead them out. The rest of you will hover outside the force field so that if the crack begins to close again, you can keep it open."

"How can we be sure we won't hit one of you while we're trying to keep the tunnel open?" Alto asks.

"Partner," Pete says, "we can't be sure. You'll just have to use your radar, and hope for the best."

"It's certainly perilous," Sedge Jennings says.

"Nah," Pete says. "It'll be as easy as falling off

a log."

"I'd like to volunteer to go into the hole with you," Alto says. "I don't mind taking chances myself, but I don't like to risk hitting my own squadron mates."

"I'm glad to hear that partner," Pete says. "But I'd prefer it if you stayed outside the force field. You have terrifically fast reflexes. We can use your skills better out here, especially if the hole starts closing in and we need to get out. Now let's get going and find that weak point!"

"Hey, wait a minute," Alto says. "I know I can do more *inside* the force field. If I've got such terrifically fast reflexes, you're going to need them in there!"

"Count me in too," you say.

"Have it your way," Pete says amiably. "Now let's get started!"

You fix your eyes on the display screen as the computers work out the route each Hawk will take around the force field. As soon as your course and speed come up on the display screen, you hit the throttle and streak away from the others.

→ → → → → → → → → → → → → → → →

Go on to the next page.

Centrifugal force presses you against your restraints as your Phantom follows a curve along the edge of the force field for millions of miles. With constant electronic monitoring, you're able to keep as close to the edge as you want without crossing over. It's tense, hard work, requiring split-second timing. For a long time you get no indication of any imperfection in the field. Then your magnometer begins to quiver. Suddenly it drops to zero—you've found a crack!

You train your radar down into the fissure, quickly picking up an echo. It could be Norie or Rapper!

You position the nose of your Phantom over the crack and send out high-gain radio signals on standard Space Hawk frequencies. "Hawk 5 and Hawk 6, this is Hawk 3, do you read me?"

A few minutes later, you get a faint message back.

"This is Hawk 5. I read you, but we . . ."

Norie's message fades away. You keep signaling, but all you hear is static from magnetic interference within the force field. You've never felt so frustrated. Why did Norie's message cut out on you?

You glance at the lateral data screen that shows the change of status projections. The crack is slowly closing.

You can't radio Pete or any of the other Hawks for instructions now because their spacecraft are on the other side of the force field. No signal could reach them. And if you wait for your rendezvous with the other Hawks, the hole may be completely closed up by the time they arrive to help.

You have an urge to take your Phantom down through it while you have the chance. Time is running out.

← ← ← ← ← ← ← ← ← ← ← ← ← ← ← ←

If you dive through the crack and try to locate Norie and Rapper, turn to page 59.

→ → → → → → → → → → → → → → → →

If you rendezvous with the other Hawks and report on what you've found, turn to page 75.

With a heavy heart, you fire your maneuvering burners, one forward and one retro, swinging the Phantom around in a wide arc. You photograph the space fortress continually as you swing past your closest point of approach— about three million, five hundred thousand miles. Even with the Phantom's 600 power scope, you're unable to make out any imperfections in its smooth, gleaming surface.

The only new thing you do notice is a slight difference in color on the side of the space fortress that faces the brilliant star Procyon. You wonder if the fortress is powered by solar energy through this source. If it were, the skin might be made of photovoltaic material, which would produce a direct electrical current by chemical action, as in a battery, and that might account for the change in color where the intense light is striking it.

Other than that, you've learned nothing. Perhaps with the aid of computer-enhanced images, scientists on Earth will be able to draw some conclusions. But you can't think about that now. The Phantom is now reoriented. It's time to begin the six-minute countdown, patch in the coordinates for FTL, and return to the solar system.

← ← ← ← ← ← ← ← ← ← ← ← ← ← ← ←

Turn to page 60.

Another transmission comes in from Norie. "Hawk 3, where are you? Rapper and I have a clear shot now through the crack—we're going to make it. You've got to hurry, the crack's about to close up again!"

Then there is nothing but earsplitting static.

Your two friends reached the upper part of the crack before it closed in. You're thankful they made it out. But your fate looks very different. You're now so ensnared near the center of the force field that no maneuver, no ploy, seems to help. Like a fly in a spider's web, the more you struggle, the more hopelessly you become trapped.

→ → → → → → → → → → → → → → →

Go on to the next page.

Then through the viewport you see a multi-pronged robot, just like a spider. It's coming toward you from Gamma One, as if it were going to clear the web of its prey.

The End

You accelerate away from the crack and head for the rendezvous point. Meanwhile you radio the other Hawks that you've found an opening in the force field. Most of them won't get the message because radio waves can't penetrate the field, but as you travel around Gamma One, you're able to establish contact with several Hawks, who in turn are able to relay the message to the others. Soon, everyone in the squadron has gotten the word and is streaking back to the rendezvous point.

On the way there, a message from Igor Denisov comes over the radio. "Sedge reported that he too found a crack in the force field. I was close by, so I raced over to inspect it. I found no crack, nor any sign of Sedge! I searched everywhere, but no luck. I think Sedge got pulled into the crack, and when it closed up behind him, he got trapped."

You hear groans over the radio circuit as this news reaches the other Hawks.

"So now there are three Hawks down there," Pete says. "We'll get them out—it's just a question of finding another opening in the field. Hawk 3, give us your report again."

You tell them about your discovery, and about Norie's message. "The crack was still open when I left it."

→ → → → → → → → → → → → → → → →

Go on to the next page.

"All right, Hawk 3," Pete says, "lead us to it!"

You carefully plot the coordinates of the area where you found the crack, and have no trouble finding the spot again. But when you reach it, you find no irregularities in the magnetic lines of the force field.

The other Hawks arrive right behind you.

"The crack's completely closed up," you report.

"It's like flying over a cloud-covered land-scape," Alto says. "You see a break in the clouds, and by the time you get there it's closed up again."

"And we're like the pilot in that situation who's runnin' low on fuel," Pete says. "We don't have time now to wait for a break in the clouds. We're going to have to blast our way in. This calls for ploy 9."

The moment you hear this you bring up the ploy 9 program. Then, following the vectors that appear on your computer screen, you maneuver your Phantom along with those of the other Hawks so that all of you are converging on the same point where you had observed the crack opening earlier.

It takes several minutes before all nine Phantoms are stabilized, hovering in space, each on a heading that is precisely maintained. To make sure your laser cannons will fire in unison, the orders will be made from the computer on Pete's Phantom directly to the computers of the other Hawks.

You glance at the special display board. A green light marks each Phantom that is in proper alignment. One after another the lights come on, sometimes flickering off for a moment when the pilot wavers off course.

"All heat and light shields in place," Pete orders.

You check yours carefully—the concentrated force of energy is going to be tremendous. You have to keep maneuvering your craft, maintaining your green light continuously. In a few moments nine green lights—one for each Phantom—are visible on screen.

→ → → → → → → → → → → → → → → →

Go on to the next page.

You fire, along with the other Hawks.

A tremor rocks your spacecraft. The instruments showing magnetic lines of force wave wildly, as if they're being pounded by a hammer. The image on your screen is blinding—light more than ten thousand times brighter than the midday sun.

It takes a few moments for the instruments to settle down. The light intensity meter begins to fall rapidly.

Alto's voice is the first to sound in your earphones. "Wha-hoo! We did it! We blew it wide open! I'm going in."

"I'm glad you're coming," Pete says. "But you'll have to follow me, partner. Hawks 9, 10, and 12, lay back. If we get stuck in there, we'll need you to open it up again. Now all you Hawks going in—make sure you're back here within twelve minutes. I don't want to risk the crack closing in on us while we're scattered all over the place."

Your display screen shows the other Phantoms streaking through the opening in the force field. You're right behind them! Once inside, you peel off in search of the trapped Hawks. You know the crack won't stay open long—you'll only have a few minutes to find them.

→ → → → → → → → → → → → → → → →

Turn to page 80.

There's still a great deal of electromagnetic disturbance in this region. Less than a minute after entering the force field, you lose radio contact with the other Hawks. Your instruments indicate interference, but the computer seems sluggish in processing the data.

You continue farther into the field, but it's getting more and more impossible to navigate. You're worried you won't be able to find your own way out, much less rescue anyone else!

You watch every sensor, transmitting on every possible frequency that Norie, Sedge, and Rapper might be monitoring, hoping you'll find one of them. You glance at your clock. Time is running out—only two minutes left to get back, and not a single sign of them.

You turn in a wide loop, checking and rechecking your course and speed, trying to get on a heading that will take you back to the opening. But you have a feeling you may be on the wrong course. The instruments are quivering, and so are you.

Then your jaw falls open. Gamma One is clearly visible through the starboard viewport! You've been going in the wrong direction—you're headed toward the very center of the force field!

Gamma One is surprisingly small—not more than several hundred feet long. It's blimp

shaped, and seems to be perfectly smooth, except for two sets of spire-shaped antennae. Your computer analyzes that one of them is pointed directly toward the swarm of Cephids, some six light years away. The other is pointed toward the star Vega.

→ → → → → → → → → → → → → → →
Go on to the next page.

82

You've discovered a valuable piece of information. It seems almost certain now that Gamma One is controlling the Cephids. It also seems possible that Gamma One itself is controlled by a source near Vega. You only wish you could radio this data to the other Hawks, but there's no chance of getting a message through from deep inside the force field.

You're in grave trouble now, unable to communicate to the other Hawks, or even to navigate your Phantom properly.

But this could be a golden opportunity! Your laser cannon still has plenty of reserve energy. You're so close to Gamma One right now, there's a chance you could actually destroy it. On the other hand, if Gamma One has some kind of advanced inner defense, you might only provoke it to turn on you! Maybe you should just continue your search for the other Hawks.

→ → → → → → → → → → → → → → → →

If you decide to blast away at Gamma One,
turn to page 85.

If you decide to continue looking for the other
Hawks, turn to page 89.

You have a strong feeling that you better get out of here, and fast. You switch on your stealth shield and swerve sharply to port, then direct the computer to steer a zigzag course away from the alien object. At the same time you apply extra power in short bursts, making your Phantom a more difficult target.

Gamma One is not firing at you, but in less than a minute your sensors report increasing magnetic disturbances. The force field is closing in again!

The computer estimates that it will take three more minutes to reach the perimeter of the field, based on your present rate of speed.

That may not be enough time. Your stealth shield and zigzagging are holding you back. You drop the shield, deactivate the evasive program, and apply full emergency power. You almost pass out as terrific g forces flatten you against your seat.

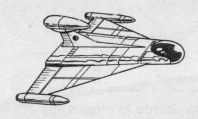

→ → → → → → → → → → → → → → → →

Turn to page 91.

You quickly radio a response. "Hawk 6, this is
Hawk 3. I read you. What's your location?"

"Bearing 22-88-120," Sedge Jennings says.

"Follow us!" This last voice is Norie's.

Then you see them, about twenty miles ahead
of you, climbing and gaining speed. Within moments they're even farther ahead of you. You
raise your Phantom's nose and fire your auxili-
ary thrusters. As your spacecraft accelerates,
you're jammed back into your seat.

A moment later your instruments are working
again. You've reached the opening in the force
field—your one route of escape. As you pass
through it, magnetic interference fades to zero.
Then you pick up Norie and Rapper and Sedge
and several other Hawks on radar. A few minutes later the entire squadron is back on station.

"Hope you've all enjoyed yourselves." It's Pete
Walton. "I think we've spent enough time around
here, partners," he says. "Begin the countdown
for FTL mode."

You grin with relief when you hear this order.
With a little luck you'll be back in Hawaii within
a couple of days.

→ → → → → → → → → → → → → → → →

Turn to page 93.

This is an opportunity you can't pass up. You head your Phantom toward Gamma One.

As you approach the strange, blimp-shaped object, you keep an eye on the range finder and read off the numbers.

Eight thousand miles, seven thousand, six thousand, five thousand, four thousand . . .

Your body tenses with excitement. You never thought you could get this close! But then you frown. The electronic sensors are registering a sharp increase in ambient magnetic energy. The video image of Gamma One shows that a dish-shaped structure near its nose is turning toward you.

→ → → → → → → → → → → → → → → →

Go on to the next page.

You'd like to get even closer, but you know you better not try. You flip the safety guard off of a tiny lever marked Full Laser Fire—Magnum Blast, uncovering a thumbsized, red plastic disc normally hidden from view. You touch it.

A tremendous laser beam surges out of your cannon—every ounce of concentrated energy the Phantom can deliver. No shield should be able to withstand such power at this close a range!

Your instruments swing wildly. All readings are off the scale. Your video monitors show nothing but dancing patterns of light. Then everything returns to normal. Magnetic activity drops almost to zero. You've broken up the force field!

As your video screen clears, you expect to see only charred wreckage and pieces of Gamma One. However, the strange, blimp-shaped object is still in place, and there's not a scratch on it. What's more, the dish-shaped structure near its nose is still trained directly on you!

→ → → → → → → → → → → → → → → →

Go on to the next page.

It will take at least several minutes more before your laser cannon recharges. Meanwhile you feel like a sitting duck. You quickly scan your sensors, and gain one new piece of information. Gamma One is sending a coded sequence of radio signals toward the star Vega. It's not hard to guess it's a message about your attack!

You've got a fast decision to make. The force field is down, at least for the moment. That means the Hawks trapped inside should have no trouble escaping. You should have no trouble either, unless you're destroyed by Gamma One.

You might have time to recharge your laser cannon and strike another blow. Your range is closer than ever now. This time you might succeed in destroying it.

Should you try to make evasive maneuvers until your laser cannon is recharged, then attack Gamma One again? Or should you just try to get away?

→ → → → → → → → → → → → → → → →

If you maneuver and then attack,
turn to page 109.

← ← ← ← ← ← ← ← ← ← ← ← ← ← ← ←

If you try to get away, turn to page 83.

You continue on, searching blindly for an opening in the force field. You keep sending out radio signals, but it's hard to imagine the other Hawks could get through the magnetic storms whirling around you.

Then the area ahead of you is filled with a swirling, pinkish gas. You're going so fast there's no time to avoid it!

Your guess is that the gas cloud is caused by radiation striking free-floating neutrons. You raise your radiation shields just seconds before you enter it.

→ → → → → → → → → → → → → → → →

Go on to the next page.

A red flashing light comes over the Geiger counter. The radiation rate is climbing. You watch in horror as it passes the danger level.

Checking off emergency procedures in your mind, you try to think about what you can do. You can't take this level of radiation much longer. But there's nothing you can do now— nothing.

You close your eyes for a moment, then open them in a hurry. The radiation counter has suddenly stopped clicking. You're out of the cloud!

"Hello, Mate, how's it going?"

You can hardly believe your ears. It's Rapper!

← ← ← ← ← ← ← ← ← ← ← ← ← ← ← ←
Turn to page 84.

The Phantom performs the way it's supposed to. In just thirty-six seconds you reach the perimeter of the force field. A minute more and you've established radio contact with the other Hawks, including Norie, Rapper, and Sedge, who managed to escape from the force field minutes earlier, thanks to you!

When Pete Walton learns that it was a magnum blast from your laser cannon that broke up the force field, he flies close by, dipping his fins in the Space Hawks salute.

"I'm proud to be flyin' with you, partner," he says. Then he sends a message to all Hawks on the open channel. "Begin countdown for FTL transit. We're heading home."

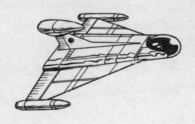

→ → → → → → → → → → → → → → →
Go on to the next page.

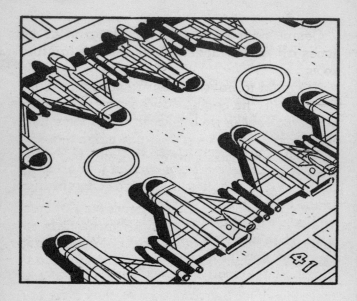

Within a few days, you and the rest of the squadron touch down safely in Hawaii, your rescue mission successfully completed. The Hawks are now back at full strength.

→ → → → → → → → → → → → → → →

Go on to the next page.

Commander Bradford's face is grim as he faces all twelve Space Hawks in the briefing room.

"It's good to have our entire squadron back here again," he begins. "Those days and nights when our Hawks were trapped in the force field were some of the worst I've known. I'm thankful you were able to rescue them. I wish we could celebrate, but I'm sorry to report that we've received more bad news. As you know, we'd hoped to get help in our defense against the Cephids. The Fiber People are more advanced than we are, and we thought they could be of some help to us. They weren't hostile, but they weren't friendly either. When one of our Hawks visited them to ask for help and advice, they gave neither."

"What about the Baakrans?" Pete asks.

"The news about the Baakrans is the worst of all," Bradford says. He looks over toward Maria Marquez, Hawk 8, who led the team on a recent mission to Baakra. "Maria, would you give your report?"

Maria hops up on the platform. She begins, "Since the Baakrans have stopped fighting with one another, we had hopes that they would cooperate with us in their defense against the Cephids."

→ → → → → → → → → → → → → → → →

Go on to the next page.

"When our team left there just over a week ago," Maria continues, "we told them not to fight the Cephids, but to wait until we could send our whole squadron there to help them. I assured them that we would arrive before the Cephids got close to their planet. Unfortunately, they didn't follow our advice. Z'bong, the red-furred commander, led twenty fighters out into deep space. He tried to scare off the Cephids by launching an attack on them before they got any closer to the planet. But when his fighters fired on the Cephids, these creatures, as we know, were not only unharmed but actually gained in size and power. Z'bong and his entire squadron were destroyed within hours."

A murmur of voices fills the room. Maria's report is indeed bad news.

"We'd better take off for Baakra pretty soon then," Stefan Svensen says.

At that moment a staff officer hurries into the room and hands a computer printout to Maria. She shakes her head as she reads it.

"We're too late," she says, scanning the message onto the screen.

The mesage is from Zeldus, commander of the green-furred Baakrans.

To Earth from Baakra: The Cephids have landed. They are destroying everything, growing larger and stronger. Thousands

more arrive on the planet with each minute. Baakra is doomed. You tried to help us, and we thank you.

We are sending this message from the only base we have left. At this very moment more Cephids than we can count are coming toward us across the plain.

Farewell, good people of Earth, and good luck.

→ → → → → → → → → → → → → → →

Go on to the next page.

There is a stunned silence when Maria finishes reading this message. You can't help but feel sorry for the people of Baakra. The idea of a plague that wipes out an entire planet is horrifying. And with Baakra destroyed, the leading edge of the Cephid horde must now be headed toward Earth.

"What hope is there for us?" Sedge Jennings says, finally breaking the silence.

"Good question," Igor Denisov replies. "How much use can it be to have the best space force in the galaxy when we're up against an enemy like this?"

"The deck is really stacked against us," Jack Tyner says. "If we score a hit on one of these monsters, we're worse off than if we missed."

Commander Bradford, who has been listening attentively to the conversation, holds up his hand for silence. "Before you despair," he says, "we do have some good news. Doctor Bruno Vivaldi, our expert on interspecies communication, has learned a great deal from observing the baby Cephid. I see Doctor Vivaldi now, coming in through the side entrance. He's going to speak to you now."

A trim, elderly man, Doctor Vivaldi hops up onto the platform at the front of the room, leading the baby Cephid behind him! The Cephid has grown about three times its size since it was first captured. Doctor Vivaldi has it tethered to

him on a steel wire leash.

Everyone watches with amazement as the creature crawls up onto the platform, moving like some kind of giant crab. The Cephid seems quite tame, though its huge claws and razorlike teeth make you more nervous than you'd like to admit.

→ → → → → → → → → → → → → → → →

Go on to the next page.

The famous scientist smiles at the audience. "This creature is tranquilized, so you needn't worry that it will charge you," he says. "It is not a robot, as some had speculated, though it does have a tiny radio receiver in its brain. This receiver is actually part of its body, the result of genetic engineering. It would be like us having not only eyes and ears, but also an organ that could receive radio waves."

"Is it receiving messages now?" you ask.

"No," says Doctor Vivaldi. He holds up a device about the size of a deck of cards. "This is a mini transmitter we were able to create in our lab. It constantly sends a jamming signal on the precise frequency at which the Cephids receive their transmissions. We've been monitoring for signals coming from Gamma One that might be intended for our little friend here, but so far there haven't been any. Apparently, such messages are sent out only rarely. Most of the time the Cephids just follow a straight course, devouring whatever lies in their path."

Commander Bradford pats the Cephid on the back of its rubbery neck, then faces the Hawks in the audience. "As you all know by now, the Cephids eat planets, destroying everything on them. To be more precise, they eat *energy*. If you fire a laser beam at them, it's like throwing bait to a shark."

"Until we understood that," Doctor Vivaldi

says, "we ran the risk of this creature growing larger and stronger, until we could no longer control it. But you can now be sure that we're careful to limit the amount of energy it receives."

"What about diverting the Cephids onto another course?" you ask.

"There is a chance," the scientist says, smiling at you. "We've found that we can lead this baby Cephid around merely by throwing hand grenades near it. It chases after the explosions like a shark chasing tasty morsels of meat. Now if we can divert one Cephid, perhaps we could divert the entire swarm of them."

"If it can be done," Bradford says, "the Space Hawks will do it!"

Three weeks pass. The Space Hawks squadron is cruising in formation just four light years from Earth. The swarm of Cephids is now only a few million miles ahead of you. Billions of them are spread out along the leading edge. Your radar scans show that they are larger and more numerous than they were before they ravaged Baakra. A quick check on your telescreen shows that that planet now looks like a huge, burned-out cinder, devoid of all life, stripped of every molecule of water and oxygen.

→ → → → → → → → → → → → → → → →

Go on to the next page.

The Hawks streak toward the oncoming horde. This time there's none of the usual chatter back and forth. The task ahead demands intense concentration. The plan is to lay out a line of explosions ahead and slightly to the side of the Cephids.

Pete Walton's voice comes through your earphones. "All right, partners, arm your missiles and proceed to stations."

You raise the stick, applying additional power on the under thrusters. Your Phantom accelerates sharply.

You take a bearing on a couple of bright stars, Antares and Spica, then steady your course. Your display screen shows each of the other Hawks moving toward a new position. In a few minutes everyone is on station, only a few thousand miles from the nearest Cephids.

"All Hawks fully armed," Pete commands. "Shields down . . . Stand by . . . Fire!"

Your finger comes down on the missile launcher, and a tiny projectile roars out of the tube, streaking toward its target. You watch the rocket on the monitor to confirm that it's on course, then you steeply bank and reverse direction.

Barely a minute later, the multimegaton nuclear warhead explodes. Farther out in space, toward the edge of the galaxy, other gigantic blasts go off, one after another.

Though you're thousands of miles away from

the nearest explosion, you raise all shields and filters, protecting you and the Phantom's instruments against the tremendous blasts and radiation.

Of course you don't look at the explosions directly, only at the simulated images on the computer screen. Then your eyes fix on the radar scans, the data displays that show the Cephids' course headings second by second.

→ → → → → → → → → → → → → → → →

Go on to the next page.

Exactly two minutes after the first blast, the leading Cephids begin to alter their direction. Others follow a weaving course, as if they are trying to reorient themselves. Within the next five minutes the entire swarm has altered course, now heading toward the site of the first explosion.

"They're going for it!" Pete says on the open circuit.

"I read a sixteen-degree course change!" Norie says.

You glance at your celestial chart, then speak into the open circuit. "Even if they don't alter course anymore, they'll still pass a long way from Earth, without even brushing the solar system!"

"Good job, partners," Pete says. "The Cephids are no longer a threat to Earth. Begin the FTL countdown—we're going home."

Six minutes later you and the other Phantoms enter the space-time continuum.

It seems like no time at all has passed before your spacecraft is once again gliding through the Earth's atmosphere. In a few minutes you'll be setting down in Hawaii. You've never felt happier—the Space Hawks have successfully diverted the Cephids onto a course that will take them right out of the galaxy!

When you step out of your Phantom, a huge

crowd is waiting to greet all of you. There's no doubt about it—you and the other Space Hawks are heroes!

After the welcoming ceremony, Brock Bradford calls the squadron together. With a big grin on his face the commander takes his usual position next to the holographic projector.

→ → → → → → → → → → → → → → → →

Go on to the next page.

"You're all going to get a good, well-deserved vacation beginning today," he begins. "You'll have to be back here soon, however. I received a call from the president of the Earth Federation. Each of you is going to be awarded the gold medal of honor. The ceremony will be held one month from today!"

Everyone claps.

"Let's hear it for our commander," Pete Walton calls out.

"Commander," you ask when the clapping dies down, "do you have any idea what our next assignment will be, after we get back from vacation?"

The grin fades from Bradford's face. "I can't answer that exactly," he says eventually, "but I would guess it will have something to do with the Fiber People. Shortly before you left for your last mission, our astronomers on Mauna Kea reported that the space fortress is headed directly toward Earth. Before it gets here, we're going to need all twelve of you Space Hawks back in your Phantoms, ready to blast off."

The End

The meeting at Space Hawks Headquarters goes quickly. Soon afterward you and the rest of Team C—Norie Kiasaka, Jack Tyner, Rapper McCoy, and Stefan Svensen—take off, headed for deep space. Once you pass the orbit of Neptune, you prepare to go into FTL mode for the long trip to the radio source called Gamma One.

Rapper, who has been appointed team leader, begins the countdown. Six minutes later you transit—passing out of space-time and emerging almost five light years from Earth. Now, just half a million miles from Gamma One, you train all sensors on the strange radio source.

You're glad to see the other Hawks showing up on your radar screen. The technology of faster-than-light speed isn't fully understood. There's a great deal of uncertainty, and always a chance one of you won't make it through.

"Greetings, mates." You smile as you hear Rapper's voice. "We'll head straight for Gamma One. Maintain separation of at least twenty miles."

You set your course directly. Then, as you're working over your instruments, Rapper's voice comes in again. "I can't pick up any image of it, mates. Any of you having any luck?"

"This is weird," says Jack Tyner. "We should be able to magnify the object on our screens."

→ → → → → → → → → → → → → → → →

Go on to the next page.

"Maybe it's miniaturized," Norie says.

"Not that much," Jack replies.

You study the patterns on your oscilloscope, then radio the other Hawks. "We can't see Gamma One because there's a force field around it. My instruments show it's incredibly strong. We won't be able to penetrate even at full power!"

"My instruments confirm the same thing," Rapper says a moment later. "Let's fan out and cruise around the perimeter of the field. Maybe we can find a crack, or some other kind of opening. Return to this point within an hour."

You acknowledge this order, then set out on your own course, following an arc around the perimeter of the force field. You concentrate every second, wanting to get as close as possible in order to spot any breaks or cracks in the field. But if you get too close, magnetic disturbances could jam your instruments, knocking them out. One slip and you could be trapped.

You cruise on, searching as carefully as you can. Nothing turns up, and you're forced to return to the rendezvous point empty-handed. Stefan Svensen is already there. The two of you wait, your Phantoms drifitng slowly in space, expecting Norie and Rapper to arrive any minute.

An hour passes, then another; there's still no sign of either of them. Because of the force field, there's no way you can reach them by radio, or search for them near Gamma One.

"I think I know what happened," you radio Stefan. "They must have observed some kind of crack in the field and went in to investigate. The crack probably closed up, and they're trapped inside."

"What do we do?" Stefan asks. "Should we try to blast an opening and go in after them?" He sounds a lot more nervous than a Space Hawk is supposed to. You can't blame him though; you feel the same way.

"It's too risky," you say. "I think we'd better return to Earth and get help."

→ → → → → → → → → → → → → → → →

Go on to the next page.

FASTER THAN LIGHT...

Stefan agrees, and within a few minutes the two of you are preparing for FTL transit.

Soon you're back on Earth, bringing the bad news that Norie and Rapper are trapped in a force field seventeen light years away!

← ← ← ← ← ← ← ← ← ← ← ← ← ←
Turn to page 44.

You climb steeply, then suddenly dive. As you pull out, you veer sharply in one direction, then another. If Gamma One opens fire, you're not going to be an easy target!

At the same time you work your way toward the strange, blimp-shaped object. The next time you fire, you want to be so close that no shield in the galaxy could withstand the blast.

Your laser cannon is recharging rapidly. You watch the ammeter impatiently, waiting for the ready light to come on.

Suddenly every instrument in the cockpit goes wild. The entire spacecraft vibrates. Your body tingles as if charged with electricity. A high-pitched sound squeals in your ears, and your hands shake so much you can't grip the controls.

→ → → → → → → → → → → → → → →

Go on to the next page.

It wouldn't matter if you could. The force field has strengthened a hundredfold, and your Phantom is securely trapped, as if it had been encased in an enormous block of ice. You're an easy target now for the laser blast from Gamma One. It cuts through your shields like a knife through butter.

The End

EDWARD PACKARD is a graduate of Princeton University and Columbia Law School. He developed the unique storytelling approach used in Choose Your Own Adventure books while thinking up stories for his children, Caroline, Andrea, and Wells.

ABOUT THE ILLUSTRATOR

DAVE COCKRUM studied at Southern Illinois University and Colorado State University, then rounded it off with six years in the U.S. Navy. In the early seventies, he designed model kits for Aurora, and has worked for over twenty years as a comic-book illustrator at both Marvel and DC Comics, drawing such diverse titles as *Batman*, *The Legion of Super Heroes*, *Star Trek*, and *Ms. Marvel*. He is best known as the cocreator of the new *X-Men*, and for his graphic novel, *The Futurians*. Mr. Cockrum currently lives and works in the Catskill region of New York.

Choosy Kids Choose

CHOOSE YOUR OWN ADVENTURE

- ☐ 26157-6 JOURNEY TO THE YEAR 3000
  Super Edition #1 $2.95
- ☐ 26791-4 DANGER ZONES Super Edition #2 $2.95
- ☐ 26965-5 THE CAVE OF TIME #1 $2.99
- ☐ 27393-0 JOURNEY UNDER THE SEA #2 $2.95
- ☐ 26593-8 DANGER IN THE DESERT #3 $2.50
- ☐ 27453-8 SPACE AND BEYOND #4 $2.50
- ☐ 27419-8 THE CURSE OF THE HAUNTED
  MANSION #5 $2.50
- ☐ 23182-0 SPY TRAP #6 $2.50
- ☐ 23185-5 MESSAGE FROM SPACE #7 $2.50
- ☐ 26213-0 DEADWOOD CITY #8 $2.50
- ☐ 23181-2 WHO KILLED HARLOWE
  THROMBEY? #9 $2.50
- ☐ 25912-1 THE LOST JEWELS #10 $2.50
- ☐ 27053-2 VAMPIRE EXPRESS #31 $2.50

Bantam Books, Dept. AV8, 414 East Golf Road, Des Plaines, IL 60016

Please send me the items I have checked above. I am enclosing $_____
(please add $2.50 to cover postage and handling). Send check or money
order, no cash or C.O.D.s please.

Mr/Ms _____

Address _____

City/State _____ Zip _____

AV8-7/91

Please allow four to six weeks for delivery.
Prices and availability subject to change without notice.

CHOOSE YOUR OWN ADVENTURE

☐ 26983-6　**GHOST HUNTER #52** $2.99

☐ 27565-8　**SECRET OF THE NINJA #66** $2.99

☐ 26723-X　**SPACE VAMPIRE #71** $2.50

☐ 26725-6　**BEYOND THE GREAT WALL #73** $2.50

☐ 26904-6　**LONG HORN TERRITORY #74** $2.50

Bantam Books, Dept. AV, 414 East Golf Road, Des Plaines, IL 60016

Please send me the items I have checked above. I am enclosing $_____ (please add $2.50 to cover postage and handling). Send check or money order, no cash or C.O.D.s please.

Mr/Ms _____

Address _____

City/State _____ Zip _____

AV–7/91

Please allow four to six weeks for delivery.
Prices and availability subject to change without notice.

CHOOSE YOUR OWN ADVENTURE®